Donal agus Jimmy

P.D. Singer

ROCKY RIDGE BOOKS

Donal *agus* Jimmy
Copyright © 2011 by P.D. Singer
Cover Art by P.D. Singer

Published by:
Rocky Ridge Books
P.O. Box 6922
Broomfield, CO 80021

ISBN-13: 978-1-62622-000-3

First print edition: Rocky Ridge Books 2013
Second e-edition: Rocky Ridge Books, July, 2012
First Torquere Press e-Edition: October 2011 Printed in the USA as Maroon: Donal *agus* Jimmy

Praise for *Donal* agus *Jimmy*

"...smoothly flowing story with likeable characters and an incredibly strong sense of time and place. Warmly recommended."
—*Reviews by Jessewave*

"Despite the fact that the book fits its bounds so well, despite the breadth of topics covered, I would have liked more, it's impossible not to want more when something is this well written. I don't know P.D. Singer's work–I believe this is her first gay historical–but if she writes another I will be snapping it up immediately.

I recommend this book highly, and I'm sure you will enjoy it."
—*Erastes, Speak Its Name*

Best of 2011 —*Tom, Bear on Books*

Best of 2011 —*Lisa, Top2Bottom Reviews*

For Eden, who has always insisted, "You can do it!" and for the MU, who holds the fort while I'm doing it.

Donal agus Jimmy

P.D. Singer

Chapter One

THE TRAM DROPPED Donal Gallagher at the head of the street, though he did not trudge on toward home. He stepped aside to let the other workmen, tired as he, scatter around the modest neighborhood of terraced houses. Much emptier now, the tram rolled on, silently save for the bell. The Belfast City Tramway had converted to electricity only a few years ago. Donal missed neither the odors nor the turds the tram horses had left behind, not that there weren't plenty from other traffic. Ah, progress.

Instead, he turned back the way he'd come, gazing toward the shipyard. Enormous even at the distance of miles, the Arrol Gantry's girders caught enough of the evening's sunlight to shimmer. One half of the gantry looked empty, though Donal knew it was not—the ship within was still in the keel-and-ribs stage, only half plated. The other side was full and beyond full, though tomorrow it would be empty again. After a busy two years, Harland and Wolff's Ship 401 would meet the water for the first time.

Not, Donal thought with satisfaction, that it would be ready for any voyage. He had far too much work to do first. He, and of course the thousands of others who worked at the yard, would have many months of steady work and steady pay before that ship would leave the Belfast Lough, like her sister, Ship 400, had done, just yesterday.

Donal and a few others watched for the *Olympic's* return from her sea trials. Four funnels and upper decks moved magically past terraces of houses, the rest of the ship and its tugs too low in the water to be seen.

"D' ye fancy taking the grand tour tomorrow?" asked the only stranger in a sea of familiar faces. Donal glanced over, liking what he saw a bit too much—reddish gold hair beneath a flat cap peeking out just a little farther than Donal's did, and him overdue for a barbering. That hair had grown closer to the stranger's collar over the last month—Donal had watched from the pay line every Friday for weeks now. The man might have been there far longer, but Donal had only noticed him recently, standing two lines over waiting for a pay packet that had to begin with "H". Twelve thousand men drew their wages every week at Harland and Wolff—if they didn't work in the same shop or on the same section of a ship, Donal would never meet most of them. Sailing through the queue, he'd had something to dream about. He dragged his eyes back to the ship, which was drawing nearer the gantry.

"Do I fancy spending two days' pay to see a ship I've been in and out of for months?" Donal lifted his brow at the absurdity.

"Two?" The stranger regarded him frankly, which made Donal want to squirm. "I'd have thought—"

He chopped off the appraisal of Donal's status in the yard, though what he'd said already was both rude and flattering. The five shilling fee would have been the best part of two days' wages for an unskilled laborer, but part of Donal's skills were in ciphering and fore-thought. "One for the tour, one for the wage they'd dock me for missing work. Ye must figure that in too."

The stranger laughed. "That would account for the lightness of my pay packet last week. 'Twas a dear cup of tea, then, and all for me getting thirsty before end of day."

"Boiling can," Donal recited, glumly noting the offence as it would appear in the shipyard's fine book. "Half day's wage." He'd made the mistake but once—the drain on his pocket had been painful.

"Quarter day only, but still, it should have been whiskey for the price." The stranger licked his lips, a gesture Donal caught from the corner of his eye and regretted seeing. His sturdy work pants would only disguise his reaction so much— he stared fiercely at the barely moving funnels instead.

"So, you've been aboard so often you're weary of the leviathan?" the stranger jested. "Even if it has such won-ders as hot water from a tap? Or so I hear, scarce believable though it is."

"Only in first class, but quite true." Donal tried to imagine what life would be like with such a thing. He could barely imagine *en suite* facilities; his own room had a thunder mug that he never used, preferring to brave all but the worst storms to go out back to the small house, though the ewer and bowl were serviceable enough for washing and shaving. "But even second and third class cabins have washstands with running water. All three of the Olympic class ships will."

"Pull the other one." The view blocked by another tram coming up the street, the stranger gave off looking at the distant ship. "How do you know?"

Given no choice about eye contact if he were to maintain his manners, Donal tried to look at the stranger's nose instead, for if he were to notice how blue his companion's eyes were in the soft evening light.... "I cannot tell you how many washstands I've put on that ship, so if the fitters have done their work, the passengers could have as much water inside the ship as outside it." Donal could tell exactly how many washstands, both first class and second, he'd made, but shouldn't brag, and the stranger's nose was short with just the hint of an upturn...

"Sounds a dreadful idea, the way you've put it." Cripes—now he was smiling, laughing. Donal wanted to kiss him there and then, but what a scandal that would be, so he laughed instead.

"A dreadful idea indeed, even if it were hot."

"Now, I—" the stranger managed to say, "am an expert when it comes to hot water, though my hot water is for nothing so dandified as a wash. *My* hot water—" he placed fingertips upon his chest and refused to acknowledge the head shakes and snorts from the men alighting from the tram, "—makes the ship go."

"And how clever is that?" Donal mock-marveled. He would like to place his own hand where the stranger's was, but made no move, and told his face to make no sign of it. Not on a street corner. Nor anywhere in Ireland, were he wise.

"'Tis twenty nine-boilers of cleverness for each ship, though I cannot claim them all meself." The stranger put out a hand. "Jimmy Healy, boilermaker."

Donal took the offered greeting with the merest hesitation of preparation. "Donal Gallagher, joiner."

"Well met, Donal." Jimmy released his hand slowly. "I should let you get home to the family."

"My landlady will hold the meal 'til her man and I are home, but no family waits." Nor would family ever wait, unless Donal moved back with his parents and whatever of his brothers and sisters remained, and that he hoped never to do. "Though your own must long for you."

"Not so's you'd notice. My uncle courts a smiling lass, who smiles rather more on me, therefore he smiles at me not at all. And since he means to be wed soon, I search for different lodgings. What lies on this street?" Jimmy glanced to the right.

The chit *would* smile at Jimmy—Donal wished he could. "Terraced houses, two up, two down. I live that way." Donal beckoned Jimmy to come along. "There may be something farther up, though I've seen no notices."

That was nearly a lie, for he'd been given his own notice, that half of his room must be let. His father's letter crackled in his pocket, warning him that his life would shortly become a constant trial, for what else could he do but make things right at home? All their lives balanced on the razor's edge and he'd been given a sharp flick.

May 28, 1911

My dear and loving son Donal,

The family continues well, though your sister is most distressed. She's been sacked from the linen mill, they've said she's spoiled two reels, but she swears not, that's there's a young woman jealous and looking to cause trouble. I wouldn't doubt it, her young man does draw the girls' eyes, and it will be time yet before they can wed...

Kitty's young man drew Donal's eye too—that would be trouble of a different sort. He could have heard this news at Sunday dinner, but he had no doubt his father wished to make a point without asking aloud. Without Kitty's wage, low as it was, the family would be in trouble ere long, especially if Gran died and they lost her Old Age Pension. Donal would not be able to make up that five shillings a week on top of Kitty's lost wage without giving up the freedom of his own lodgings completely. Gran had made it through the winter, though, and Kitty might yet find other work, though pray Jesus not at the cotton mill. He did not want his sister to end her days young, coughing up bloody foam.

The red brick rows of attached dwellings butted up to the sidewalk on either side, letting the life of the neighborhood tumble out. Mothers called to children through open doors that let out the scents of cooking onion and cabbage. Running to answer, the small ones waved at Donal and his companion while abandoning their games and hoops. The bell of another tram jangled, and the clatter of the offloading men rang behind them.

"Where Uncle and I live now is not so different," Jimmy noted. "Were it not for the shutters and a sign or two, I might mistake your home for mine and set your landlady at sixes and sevens."

Perhaps not. And I wish ye to be there. He was aghast at his musings—Jimmy was a stranger! What was he thinking? A stranger who would be horrified to know what Donal thought of silky hair under flat caps, blue eyes with jokes lurking back of the lashes, and bodies that wore twill trousers, boots, and tweed jackets with patches on the elbows. "I have the back bedroom; the young Deegans are grown and gone, so Mrs. Deegan let me the room and boards me."

"Sounds a treat." Jimmy stopped to read a sign in a front window, but it was a political poster, not a "To Let" notice. "I'd be fortunate to find such a place. Some of the other chaps in the boiler works have offered a share in their digs, but being the fourth in the room is too much good fellowship for me."

A room to himself was a luxury, Donal knew, unnecessary expense and the cause of much clucking at home. "Ye could be saving the money toward the day ye could wed, son," his mother said at least once a month. If she only knew... He did not plan to wed, nor did he worry overmuch what people would think. Did everyone not know three dozen men, or five dozen if one counted the women, all ten, twenty, or even thirty years older than himself, who had never entered that blessed state? True, 'twas mostly those without a trade, but was he not poor as they once he'd sent money home? If anyone wished to gossip on a joiner in his sixth year as journeyman at the biggest shipbuilder in Belfast bein' a single man, he would tell them of his great love of his family, all seven of them, especially wee Annie, so sweet-natured in spite of her withered arm.

Sweet Annie and the others needed to eat, and if it were not to be potatoes or gruel for every meal, Donal would have to provide. If he could not coax more money out of Harland and Wolff, and he could not, then he'd have to make the money he had go further. And if it were madness to share quarters with a chance met acquaintance, would it not be worse madness to share with someone who knew him, who could spread the tales to those who cared, should his secret slip out? It might be for only a short while, until Kitty found work. Donal put his pay-line dreams to the darkest corner of his mind.

"Is there a pub on this street?" Jimmy interrupted his thoughts. "Ye might join me for a pint after your supper, tell me more on whatever I might find."

"The Cliffs of Moher is at the end of the road—I'll meet you there." Donal seldom visited the pub except of a payday, but would make an exception for Jimmy. How else would he get another glimpse? He touched his cap and dared a smile, but fled into the modest dwelling in the center of a row of eight, rather than watch Jimmy stroll away.

Once seated at the plank table and grace had been said, Donal laid out his troubles and his solution. "Mrs. Deegan, would it be a great bother to have another at the table? My family has had a bit of a setback; money will be tight for a while, and if we moved one of the old bedsteads into my room and I share the rent...?"

"Have you someone in mind?" Mrs. Deegan didn't even pretend to consult Mr. Deegan, who had never been heard to say "Boo!" to his wife, and indeed, didn't look up from his plate.

"Jimmy Healy, the boilermaker, from the yard." In one sentence, Donal had told her Jimmy was employed, likely to remain employed, and at what wage. He'd told her even more than he'd thought.

"Weren't some of your sister's people Healys?" she demanded. Mr. Deegan looked up with alarm, perhaps at being noticed. He nodded and hunched over his plate again.

"Is this a ginger scamp about your age?" She turned the gimlet eye back to Donal.

"I don't know how much of a scamp. Nothing in the boiler works has blown up that I recall." Jimmy had looked to be near Donal's age.

"The older brother was blond, and there's one I wouldn't give houseroom," she sniffed. "But if you can get along with him, I suppose he'll do."

If anyone gave offence, Donal feared, it would be him, not Jimmy. He finished the black pudding and boxty without choking, and bolted for the pub, muttering prayers that Jimmy had not found better lodgings already.

He had a bit of a wait, nursing the one pint he'd allowed himself, and every tiny sip brought the fresh fear that Jimmy was delayed for talking over terms with his new landlady. When the door opened to let him in, the long face he sported cheered Donal no end, until he recalled that Jimmy might not find Donal's proposition so enticing.

Swinging onto a stool without spilling a drop of the stout he'd collected, Jimmy reported, "It's been downhill since we parted," and Donal could only agree. "I've the offer of a pallet in the garret, with the boxes and bits for company, at a sum that should rent the house, or joining a household of six and minding the children evenings for part of the rent. At that, it's better than some of my other choices." Jimmy moped into his glass, giving Donal the courage to speak.

"If ye'd consider sharing a room with one man of quiet habit, with board, I'd introduce ye to the landlady."

"Only one? And meals? Donal, my new friend, if you have such a miracle in your pocket, I'd be ever in your debt!" Excitement played with doubt on Jimmy's fair brow, turned to joy an hour later (they'd had to finish their pints, mustn't do a disservice to the brew) when he'd concluded his bargain with Mrs. Deegan.

"Saturday afternoon, then, I haven't much to move." Jimmy helped Donal shove his bed against the wall and shift the wardrobe over enough that the other bedstead would fit. Their parting handshake with Jimmy's broad smile left Donal counting the days to Saturday.

That night, with his hand on his willie—testing his bed for squeaks, he was—Donal thought about the man he'd so rashly invited in and could never touch, or hint at touching, and wondered what kind of hell he'd just invented.

Chapter Two

"DID YOU SEE THE LAUNCH?" Jimmy asked, holding the headboard up for Donal to knock in the frame. "'Twas grand—down the slipway, into the water, all gentle as kiss yer hand."

Donal wished Jimmy would not even speak of kissing—working close as they were to assemble Jimmy's bed put him disturbingly near.

"Twenty tons of grease they laid on, to ease the way," Jimmy reminisced. "And down she went, into the water. All in a minute, she left a place she could never return to, to be in her own natural element. A short journey, this first, but she'll go round the world once she gets her propellers."

"Those go on in dry dock." Donal flipped the rope end to Jimmy. They wove a support for the straw mattress and featherbed, Jimmy's own, for Mrs. Deegan didn't run to that sort of generosity. Jimmy would sleep on all that luxury. Alone. Donal turned his mind from imagining two in the bed.

"Have ye no poetry in your soul for a grand ship? Is she only so many washstands to ye?" Jimmy had to be teasing—his lips turned up.

"I think about the places my washstands go." Donal had other thoughts, more poetic, but not to be shared.

"To America, or France. New York, Marseilles—I hear tell there's palm trees. The sweet, sunny port of Naples. Stockholm. My washstands go places I'll never see. Is that poetry enough?"

"I lodge with a bard," Jimmy declared, stowing his extra clothing in the wardrobe with Donal's, and hanging a small picture of his family on a nail.

They spent the rest of the day proving that not all Irishmen were bards—they sang at the session down at the Cliffs of Moher, though Donal took a friendly elbow to the ribs after his thirty-third flat note. That was fine—Donal listened to the fiddles and the singers, taking a turn with the bones and watching Jimmy make friends.

Wondering if he could make that be enough.

***

THOUGH TEMPTATION slept a few short steps away, Donal began to think he could manage. Sunday they spent apart, to his relief, which was tempered with Kitty's news that she had not yet found work. His mother accepted the handful of coin he'd brought, and must have counted in the kitchen, because her relief at the extra shillings came as a kiss on his ear as he was leaving. "You're a good son, Donal," she whispered, and her arms were tight around him.

The men lay down early, for they had to rise before sunup to catch the tram to the shipyard. Every morning, Jimmy peeked with delight into the bag Mrs. Deegan had packed with his breakfast and his dinner, which they would break work to eat at eight thirty and at one, blessing the moment he'd turned to watch the *Olympic* return from her sea trials.

"I'd be eating cold farl this morning if not for you," Jimmy'd confided that Monday.

"You'll be eating it this morning too," Donal pointed out. They each had a triangular wedge of soda bread.

"With sausage and a bit of cheese, though." Jimmy nibbled the tiny corner he'd broken off. "And it's soft and fresh, not the fluke of an anchor."

Donal had dismounted at the end of Queen's Road wondering if Mrs. Deegan's cooking would keep Jimmy around in spite of any gaffe he might make.

One of the leviathans, without funnels or upper decks, rode high in the water at the fitting dock, the huge floating crane looming over it. The other no longer dominated the shipyard—the *Olympic* had sailed away Wednesday afternoon. No one expected to see her back until she required refitting, for the Thompson Graving Dock there at the yard was the only one in the world large enough for her.

"Go make her some washstands." Jimmy touched the edge of his cap.

"Columns for a lower deck lounge first," Donal told him. "Some Turkish bath affair." Immediately he regretted mentioning a room that suggested nakedness, but Jimmy had turned toward the boiler shed, and Donal was left with his confusion.

They met again at home—Donal considered waiting at the tram stop for Jimmy only once, discarding the notion as lovesickness. Jimmy was a big boy who knew his way back; finding him in the sea of men leaving the yard at five thirty would be near impossible. And best not to find himself pressed up against Jimmy in a tram loaded full to bursting, though Donal imagined such things in the dark.

The bed had tested squeakless and a good thing, too, when he lay awake listening to Jimmy's soft breathing and thinking of the morning, when they'd have to wash, shave, and dress to be at their workbenches by six. Donal tried to keep his eyes averted then, without being obvious about doing that, or looking hopeful that Jimmy might be looking at him. Jimmy smiled a lot in the mornings, but he smiled a lot in the evenings, too, whether weeding Mrs. Deegan's garden or strolling off to fetch a newspaper or see a friend. He did not smile so much after reading the papers, nor did Donal.

Friday came—payday. Thinking the government could stand to learn a few things from Harland and Wolff, Donal buzzed through the pay-lines with twelve thousand others and still reached the tram stand by a quarter to six. He'd pay Mrs. Deegan, set aside the share for his family, and could spare the price of a pint or two. Without assurance that Jimmy would choose the local pub over his old haunts, Donal did not think the beer would have much taste.

"D'ye think they'd mind if I brought my whistle?" Jimmy improved the flavor of the beer with one question, once they'd finished their supper.

"Not near so much as they'd mind if I sang." Donal's happiness might be a big enough bucket to carry a tune.

Jimmy proved a fine player, and if the chatter in the pub didn't quiet when a new tune started, no one much expected it to. Donal kept half his attention on the lilt of a certain pennywhistle while greeting friends and neighbors, learning the news, whose nephew had a new son or whose cousin was sailing away to America, who had run afoul of the *gombeenmen*.

"Debt, it's a terrible thing," old Frankie told him. "And the Molloys still waiting on a remittance from their Artie in America."

Donal would forgive Jimmy everything the man did to his peace of mind, just for coming along at the right moment to keep his family from needing to borrow a penny from the *gombeenmen*.

Voices rose in one corner of the pub, nothing unusual, though the venom was. "Home Rule is Rome rule!" someone yelled, and stool legs screeched against the slate floor. *Not politics, not of a Friday night with a lovely pint,* Donal thought, but someone had drunk enough beer to begin a "discussion" of a change of government, a topic gaining more heat these years. "And you know Lord Pirrie supports it!"

The head of Harland and Wolff probably thought he could get a lot more concessions out of a smaller government dependent on one of the largest employers in the region and didn't have a care for Catholic or Protestant. Donal drained his glass quickly, preparing to leave before things grew heated and stools flew, but Jimmy was still deep in the music.

"I learned this from a Tyne-side fellow," Jimmy said, and started a tune with a spritely sound that cut through the argument.

"Shut yer gob, we can't hear!" A fiddler startled the political thinker into silence, letting the twitter of the whistle pierce sudden quiet that grew into mutters. "Again,

Jimmy, without the ornaments." More plainly this time, Jimmy ran through the melody, and other voices shushed the argument into sullen quiet. A fiddle joined in, then another, instruments picking up and dropping out, and Jimmy leading until everyone had the notes and began to add the rolls and trills that made the tune their own.

"Thank ye for the tune, lad." The landlord gave Jimmy a third bevvie, no doubt grateful that all the stools had remained on the floor, and escorted one of the politicians outside, whispering in his ear. Donal relaxed, wishing he hadn't been so quick to drain his glass, and let the music bring back his smile. Jimmy pulled down a draft, then wiped the foam from his lip and put the whistle to work again. Donal had to look away, and when he dared look back, it was because Jimmy had begun to sing to the tune he'd just taught them. The glass was empty—had Jimmy downed that pint in less than two minutes?

It would carry him out of the pub in a bit, but fast enough that he wouldn't cause a scene of his own? A jig began—Jimmy did some reeling as well, but heading the wrong way, whistle in hand. Donal caught him at the door, still singing.

"D' ye need the jacks?" Donal whispered.

"In a bit," Jimmy broke off to answer, then warbled again about chickens for the wedding feast, provided by the groom. "*Donal, 'se Donal, 'Se Donal a rinne an bhainis, Donal agus Morag...*" He stumbled on the rising notes of the girl's name, throwing an arm over Donal's shoulder.

"Home with ye, don't make a scene." Donal didn't care to hear his name coupled with a woman's in marriage, but Jimmy's full tenor wasn't suffering much from the beer, aside from the high notes, and his arm lay warm against the back of Donal's neck.

"Which way? *Donal agus Morag...*" Jimmy tried again, leaning heavily but letting Donal guide him out the door and down the road. If only this was not the sole reason to put an arm about Jimmy's waist.

Not the first time he'd walked a gee-eyed friend home, and Jimmy was nice about it, stumbling but giving no sign of hurling. The gardie they met halfway back might have been a problem, but "Since you're takin' him home, and that not far," they didn't add an arrest for public drunkenness to the evening. Donal heard a faint echo of *Donal agus Morag...*" from behind them.

"Your song's over," Donal shushed Jimmy after a trip out back and before the ordeal of the stairs. "Do *not* vex Mrs. Deegan!"

Jimmy quit mid-word. He still needed a bit of help up, and once into their still dark room, he toppled into the bed, so abruptly that he didn't let go of Donal's neck, nor could Donal do aught but fall with him, arm trapped.

Jimmy lay quiet as stone, and near as heavy. Donal tried to pull his arm out from under his friend, but two or three tugs convinced him he was stuck fast. It could have been far worse—trapped with his head on Jimmy's shoulder, he was at least cozy, so cozy he'd tell Jimmy that there was no getting his arm back from under a great lump of a bolloxed gingernut until he'd slept off the beer. How much had Jimmy drunk? Enough to believe the tale Donal would need to explain his hard willie? Perhaps Jimmy's noticin' wouldn't run to that, pressed up against his leg though it was. Donal relaxed to the inevitable best he could, with his free arm over Jimmy's belly. Oh, but the man was warm. He'd not worn a waistcoat and now Donal's hand lay under the tweed of Jimmy's jacket, with only a cotton shirt between them.

Thank the Lord Jimmy didn't snore. Not that Donal could sleep, all his attention being on Jimmy like that. Not all—he needed some to keep his traitor body from humping against his companion. There'd be *no* explaining that. Donal hadn't imagined a worse torment than trying to sleep across the room from Jimmy—now he cursed himself for a short-sighted fool. Quietly and repeatedly.

"If it's that bad, I'll let ye up." Jimmy didn't sound drunk at all—his murmur was clear and soft. "But I think ye're fine where ye are."

"Ye do, do ye?" Donal hissed, his body gone rigid. "What makes ye think *I* think it's fine?"

"This." Jimmy rubbed his leg against Donal's cock, and the friction, even through two pairs of trousers, was almost enough to undo him. "And it's yerself ye're cursing, not me. At least stay while we talk—voices carry."

The window was open, though it faced to the garden in back. The other houses in the terrace butted up to either side, and who knew what the neighbors might hear if their windows were open to the soft spring night? Donal stayed.

"Ye feigned drunk," Donal accused him. "Ye let me think ye were well potted." He had no idea what to do with his hand, and holding his head above Jimmy's shoulder was getting wearing.

"How else would I get your arm around me?" Damn Jimmy for sounding like the very voice of reason. "But if two pints were enough to tank me, I could not call meself an Irishman."

In truth, Donal had wondered at three. "The third?"

Jimmy chuckled. "Switched glasses with the man with the *bodhrán;* better he should drink it than play."

There was a thing that could not be argued. "But this? Ye want me to...?" Lacking words, Donal flopped back against Jimmy's side.

"This. More than this. But if ye do not, say the word; I'll let ye up, we'll say no more of it. But I do not think ye really want that, and I know I do not." Jimmy's hand had crept to Donal's forearm, and the small strokes of his rough fingers bunched and smoothed the wool. "Ye did not struggle but once or twice when we lay down together. Had ye tried harder, I would have rolled over."

"When we *fell* down together." Relieved that Jimmy was so far from anger, Donal was still stung at being duped. Yet Jimmy was right—how else would Donal's head ever come to Jimmy's shoulder? "What more do you want?"

"I don't know all the 'more' there could be," Jimmy murmured into Donal's hair. "Do you?"

"How could I?" Donal let his hand mimic Jimmy's, stroking against the ridge of muscle in Jimmy's side. "I've never had even this."

"Nor I." Jimmy moved his lips against Donal's head, brushing down his face when Donal tipped back. "But we could start with a kiss."

A kiss, yes, a kiss—was that not one of the things he'd dreamed of? Donal searched with his lips—he could feel Jimmy craning to him, yet with his arm trapped beneath, they couldn't reach.

"I must let ye go to have ye." Jimmy rolled enough to free Donal's arm, and now Donal could hitch himself up enough to lean down to Jimmy's mouth. He barely knew what to do, kisses were not part of his world, but gamely nibbled on, finding courage with every sweet nuzzle and lick. The first little wetness against his lip startled him, but if Jimmy thought this was how to do it... Donal had always been a quick study, and if tongue to lip was nice, tongue to tongue was nicer. Nicer than he'd imagined last night with his hand on his flesh. If he'd but known....

Donal forgot everything in their dance of mouths; forgot how to breathe, forgot how to still his body. Gasping, he thrust against Jimmy's hip, but that wasn't enough for either of them. Jimmy pulled him over, atop, and Donal did not know what to make of this. They were chest to chest, groin to groin, mouth to mouth, and Jimmy pressed back against him, his hands urging Donal on.

'Twas the eager hand on his bum that undid him—Jimmy gripped the big muscle, pulling Donal down to meet his own rising body, their cocks crushed together and sliding within their linens. Jimmy squeezed once more—Donal crashed down, trembling, while waves rolled through him, starting deep within some place he had no name for, squeezing out a cry. Jimmy caught that cry, swallowed it, and with a mighty heave, gave one back. They lay together, small shudders wracking their frames, breath hard come by, but returning.

"We've learned a bit about beginning," Jimmy murmured, his fingers drawing lazy trails up Donal's back.

"And quite a bit about the ending." Donal mumbled, feeling his stickiness wet against his belly. "There didn't seem to be a middle."

"Not yet." Jimmy brushed his cheek against Donal's— they rasped a tiny *scritch* in the dark. "Undressing might be part of it."

"Yes, undressing," Donal agreed dreamily, then jerked his head up. "Boots!" He swept their feet off the bedding and jumped up. Mrs. Deegan would know entirely too much if they dirtied the coverlet. He pulled off his boots, then Jimmy's, brushing at the coverlet to remove any bits of mud.

"Let's do the rest more slowly?" Jimmy rose to put his arms around Donal, who sank against him in the cover of dark, then let him slide the jacket from his shoulders to hang on the peg. They undressed each other with un-steady fingers, and spent the rest of the night finding the middle.

Chapter Three

THE FLAT OF MRS. DEEGAN'S hand against the door jerked Donal upright and out of bed. "Up with ye—the whistle's blown!

Jimmy blinked sleepy eyes, then swatted Donal's retreating arse gently. Neither stopped to shave—the dockyard would have to look at whiskers. The small pitcher of water they were expected to share had to clean the scent of each other away. They leaped into any old clothing, pelted down the stairs, fair snatching their burlap dinner bags from Mrs. Deegan's hands.

"One pint too many last night," Donal apologized from halfway out the door.

"There'll be a Temperance Pledge in this house if ye miss work for the drink!" followed them out into the street. "Even of a Saturday!"

They had to chase the tram to the next stop, which woke them entirely, and while Jimmy got a seat, Donal had to stand for the crowding, but they'd be to work on time. A half-day's separation, and perhaps some time to think, that's what they needed.

The lumberyard yielded four ash trunks, which Donal would lathe into columns for the Turkish bath, and if anyone questioned his contentment, it was for the even match and fine grain of the wood. His luck held that afternoon, too—his team won their game of Gaa, and surely Jimmy's afternoon off was going as well. The world was so sweet that even Mrs. Deegan relented and brought out the pudding when Jimmy swore to her they would not take more ha'pence to the pub than would buy them one jar each, and that they'd be home for an early evening. "To be well rested for church," he assured her, and she said nothing frightening about temperance.

She even boiled another kettle to reheat the bathwater after Mr. Deegan's wash, and Donal yielded his place as third bather to Jimmy. Being last into the galvanized tub carried the consolation of imagining Jimmy naked in the kitchen, his bare knees poking up from the water, his skin soapy. Jimmy must have had similar thoughts, for when he'd come back upstairs to dress, he kissed Donal swiftly, out of sight of the window. Luck held further—no political discussions grew loud enough to disrupt the evening at the pub, which they cut short, and when they got home and doused the light, they were luckiest of all.

***

THE ONE MORNING of the week they could indulge in a lie-in was Sunday, though Jimmy had made promise of church. "I didn't ask because it didn't matter," Donal whispered into Jimmy's well-nibbled ear. "And I only ask now because I don't know when services start."

"Church of Ireland." Jimmy played with the pale down on Donal's chest. "Ten o'clock."

"Presbyterians start at nine." The assurance had been made implicitly for him too. "I may have to convert." But nev-

er to a church who would make say him aloud that he repent-
ed of their joy, nor would he ever promise not to do it again.

Kitty had no news at Sunday dinner, but that would
have been asking for perfection in the world. Donal returned home to find Jimmy playing chess with Mr.
Deegan, and that was perfection enough.

***

JIMMY HANDED DONAL his cap. "If I come to Sunday dinner
with ye, your family will know there is something between us.
They know you too well. Or they'll catch me hangin' on every
word of a story of some bit of cleverness ye did in short pants.
Something a mere mate from the yard wouldn't care about."

"Except to tease me with later." He was disappointed,
yet still saw the wisdom of Jimmy's words.

"I don't think I could keep me face straight. We can fool
the other men—they aren't looking so closely, and with
time we need not spend so many evenings apart. People
will take it for granted that I no longer hie out to my old
haunts, but until then..." He swept a blond strand away
from Donal's brow. "Go see your family; I'll have Sunday
dinner with the Deegans."

Knowing Jimmy was right didn't console Donal at all.
"We'll turn in early."

"And sure, doesn't Monday morning come too soon?"
Sharp-eyed Kitty would see right through them if she saw
Jimmy twinkle at him like that. Donal stole a quick kiss
and left for the tram.

Far from being the instrument of detection, Kitty
proved to be Donal's great joy.

"I've found service, Donal!" she cried, almost before he'd gotten wee Annie untangled from his waist. Hoisting his youngest sister to his shoulder, such a slight burden for nine, he now had an arm to crush Kitty's news out of her. "Lighter work than the mill, and better pay!"

"Wonderful! What is it?" He envisioned long treks out to wealthy sections of the city, long hours, and could not imagine how that was an improvement.

"I'm to keep house for four. Cook, clean, and come home to sleep. And the pay! Donal, a shilling eight pence a day!" No wonder Kitty was dancing. "Sundays are dinner only, too! Oh, Donal!"

"That is an improvement!" She'd been toiling in the mill for about half that, ten hours a day. Donal suspected that the real reason she'd been let go was that some twelve year old had come knocking at the mill door, willing to work for even less. "Who will be eating your fine cooking?"

"Do ye recall Sam Ternahan and Andrew Fry?" Kitty poked Annie's nose, making her giggle. "No telling!"

Of course Donal recalled them. Sam and Andrew were great neighborhood favorites, living in a house three terraces up for as long as he could recall, and one was never far from the other. The two had taken him fishing, guided his first chess moves, and taught him more than they knew about how one man could love another, though he'd never seen them touch.

"They must be looking to their old age, because they've taken a couple of boarders. One works for the haulers, and the other a painter at the yard. I started Thursday, and so far they've been very good."

"Just don't come out all over Mrs. Deegan on them if they want a pint." Donal warned her, and she laughed, having heard stories of the old besom. They set Annie down, and Donal was lost in his family for the day.

On his way out, Kitty walked him to the tram, her arm linked in his. "Donal, there is one thing that troubles me about my new place. I was coming to put up dinner, and they...."

"They what?"

"I saw Andrew with his hand on Sam's shoulder." She blushed. "Their faces were very close."

Donal understood so much more now that Jimmy had come into his life. "Don't worry about it, Kitty. It just means they won't bother you."

"If you say so." She rested her head on his shoulder for the last few steps. His younger sister always had trusted him, unless there was a frog handy. "You won't need a boarder now."

He turned to face her, keeping an eye on the tram, still a block away. "Kitty, you give Mam half your wage, and I'll make up the rest and a bit, now that I can. You keep the rest toward your wedding. My boarder's a good one, we'll all be fine." They would all be better off, and maybe, one day, there would be a home for the two of them with a Kitty of their own.

Donal went home to Jimmy full of dreams.

***

"I'm RUNNING SHORT of new tunes to distract the hot-heads," Jimmy confided on the walk back from the pub.

27

Perfectly steady on his feet on this and all their other visits, Jimmy would wait until they'd gone upstairs and doused the light before he'd throw an arm over Donal's shoulder now. And they'd be naked, and there would be kisses, and perhaps a chuckle at Mrs. Deegan's approving looks at her two sober and industrious boarders, who never stayed out 'til all hours getting pissed.

"I'd noticed you always have something distracting when the shouting starts." Donal had his hands in his pockets, lest he reach to take Jimmy's arm.

"Have we not grown weary of politics?" Jerking a thumb at a poster in a parlor window, Jimmy sounded tired. "The shouting for Home Rule started long before we were born—we've never known days when it was not discussed at the table or over a jar."

"If they can keep us shouting, they have no need to do anything." Donal's distance from politics was longer when home was only furlongs away—he didn't want to carry this discussion into bed.

"What I fear, Donal, is that the shouting will stop and the shooting begin." Jimmy said no more, but when they reached the sanctuary of their room, he held Donal tightly for a long time before pulling him down to the featherbed.

***

DONAL LOOKED with some alarm at the header of Jimmy's newspaper, dark with spots from the January sleet. "Why are ye reading the *Irish Catholic*?"

Sitting at the table in the parlor, Jimmy didn't look up, nor, Donal hoped, did he give a serious answer. "It was the handiest weapon for fending off an Orangeman."

"More like bringing a crowd of them to question your loyalties. Jimmy, why?" Steering clear of politics was nigh impossible these days, but the shipyard was nearly unanimous in its opinions, being staffed almost entirely with Protestants. Jimmy had to go seeking this newspaper—it couldn't have been easy to find in East Belfast.

"Because it has adverts I wanted." Jimmy motioned Donal to sit across from him. "The Belfast *News-Letter* doesn't see fit to run them." Folding a page, he turned the paper for Donal to read. "All the papers have the fares to America. This one has the recruiters' adverts, where the jobs are."

Running his finger down a page with Leyland Line, White Star Line, and Cunard's offers to take him to the corners of the world, Donal noted, "The fares have all gone up since the boilermakers' strike, too." Jimmy had been home with no pay for a week that summer, the shop having struck in sympathy for the workers in Liverpool protesting low pay and long hours.

"I know. Donal, you said once that you dreamed of the places your washstands go. I dream of going..." Jimmy paused so long Donal wondered if all he wanted was to get away. "I want to see for myself—one of them must be a place where a striver can get ahead. America, yes, or Australia, but where else?"

"You should have gone to sea then." Donal had never seriously imagined leaving Ireland. The ships visited vague ports in his mind, and now Jimmy had one foot on deck?

"I will." The words might have been a blow for what they did to Donal's stomach. "They need boiler repair on the steamships." He flipped the page over, and Donal left him to it, trudging upstairs alone.

He should have damped the gas lamp before he'd lain down: the sun had risen when they'd broken work for breakfast and had set before the end of their work-day, but Donal was too tired of the dark to be thrifty. He did not undress—he was alone and cold, and to creep beneath the quilt in his long johns seemed entirely too prophetic. Lying on his bed, Donal tried to imagine his world without Jimmy in it. That world contained no colors, no sounds, and so the bed tipping down under Jimmy's weight surprised him.

"So solemn, Donal. Did I say I was going alone?" Jimmy leaned down to brush his lips across Donal's forehead, not forgetting a wary look at the curtained window, though frost would keep neighbors from seeing more than shadows. "I'll not go anywhere until I know how we'll be together again."

"Did you ask if I wished to go at all?" Keeping his hands off Jimmy's arms proved impossible—Donal quit trying.

"Nay, I did not, but you will. Have we not launched the best ships in the world and never even watched them kiss the water, or sail away, never mind sail with them?" His thigh was warm against Donal's side, his face not completely serious.

"The work is here and you speak a poet's dreams." The harshness in Donal's words pulled the smile away from Jimmy's lips.

"There's work anywhere for men of your skills and mine. If not in ships, then in cities where they have steam-heated buildings and wish for fine chairs to sit on. Or the railroads. Every locomotive needs its boilers looked to."

Truth lay in those words, though Donal had never really considered it. "Our families are here."

"True, but does not every Irish family lie half in America? We can bring the ones who will come once we're settled."

"And the ones who won't come?"

"They will see the wisdom, one day, I promise you." Jimmy cupped his hand against Donal's cheek.

"And if I don't see the wisdom?" Stubbornness born of fear made him argue.

"Then I hope you learn to like Bridget O'Brien." Jimmy took his hand back.

"And who might she be?" Donal sat up, pushing back to lean against the headboard.

"Perhaps a Pegeen Kibbard or a Jenny *Gan Ainm*, but do you think your family won't be looking to settle you down with some woman? And how will you say no, when you, journeyman joiner, make a good wage at the yard and should be bringing them grandchildren? And—" Jimmy ran his hand softly over Donal's knee. "—will any Bridget or Jenny leave room in your life for me?"

Perhaps for a game of chess or a jar at the pub, but for the rest... Donal did not even trouble to answer. He wondered how Sam Ternahan and his Andrew had managed such things—he surely couldn't go and ask. Now he needed to feel Jimmy against his heart. Putting out his arms, he tried to tell Jimmy that no Pegeen could fill that place. Jimmy came to lean across Donal's chest, an arm wrapped around from behind.

"Don't frighten me that way." Donal rubbed his face against the straight strawberry blond locks that again needed a trim. Donal would do it for him, but later.

"Ah, Donal, that's what I love about you." Jimmy used his free hand to slide under Donal's shirt. Donal froze, having never, in all these months, heard Jimmy use that word. "You see something broken, you fix it. From our first meeting, when you found lodgings for a man unwelcome in his own home, to now. But until you meet the problem, it doesn't exist for you. So I look into the future for us both."

The future Jimmy had just outlined was too frightening, and he'd said something that wasn't enough. Donal found he needed to know. "When you looked into your future eight months ago, did you see that we'd be like this now?" *I was a stranger, how could ye be certain of me?*

"I could hope. I saw ye standing, gazing at the ships, with satisfaction and maybe a dream in your eye, and thought ye handsome. The wood chip in your hair was especially fetching. I was disappointed ye'd combed it out before coming to the pub. I knew it would be a struggle to live with ye and never touch ye, but that was my life."

Donal pulled Jimmy closer—he'd expected that same life, and he hadn't known about the wood chip. "So I was the first who was ever willing." *Was I the only one who'd ever take that risk with ye?*

Jimmy's snort was loud enough to bring a faint "Bless ye!" through the closed door. With a flinch, he settled back into Donal's arms and spoke more softly yet. "Nay, I'd turned down more than one, for I couldn't trust them. Nor did I like them as I liked you. And I thought ye liked me too, for more than just... being willing."

"Don't be thick—ye know I do." Perhaps it had started that way, but now Donal could not imagine a life that didn't include his Jimmy. He tried to prove it with kisses, ardent but quiet. "It's you; not just any man will do."

Jimmy opened his mouth to catch those words.

They were the masters of stealthy movement, speedily dropping clothes to the floor. The last of the light was fading; only enough remained to see each other in outline, but Donal knew every inch of Jimmy's skin, from the lightly haired forearms to the puckered, red burn scar on his ribs, where he'd met a piece of hot metal as an apprentice some ten years ago. Donal tried to touch every dear part now, soaking Jimmy up through his own skin, from thigh to chest, with palms marked by his own trade.

Jimmy writhed against him, and the bed would have announced their pleasure to the world had it not been maintained by a professional—Donal thrust back, their cocks rubbing together until Donal could no longer stand it. "Jimmy—" he rasped, but did not know how to finish his request.

For answer, Jimmy nipped lightly at Donal's neck and swiveled around until his face lay at Donal's groin. Oh, yes, that would do—Donal took Jimmy's thick cock in his hand, slipping the skin back 'til the head lay exposed to his tongue. Wet swirls and soft licks he gave it, until he had to plunge it all into his mouth to gag the sounds Jimmy wrung from him with those same kinds of caresses.

Speed was their ally, but tonight, though Jimmy stilled and spurted, he did not try to bring Donal along. When he moved again, he went slowly, so slowly that Donal thrust against his tongue, but a soft pat at his thigh stopped him. Swiveling around between Donal's knees, Jimmy bit gently at the skin on his inner thigh, doing something with his hand.

"Shh," he cautioned before slipping Donal's cock back into his mouth, and a good thing, for the questing finger that slipped into Donal's arse would have made him yelp.

They'd played and tickled, stroked and explored, but going in was a new thing, and something they'd agreed would work much better if they had posh plumbing. Now Donal didn't care, for Jimmy had found a very good reason inside for him not to care. The darkness of the room gave way to rockets and spangles behind his clenched eyelids, and with every little press and lick, he came closer to bigger rockets below. With only enough presence of mind to pull his thin pillow over his face and let it catch the sound, Donal shuddered through his climax, whimpering again when Jimmy withdrew his finger and slid his lips over the head one last time.

Yielding his pillow, Donal pressed his face into Jimmy's chest and rested his head on Jimmy's forearm, content to nestle. No, no other man would do, and Donal wanted to fill his nostrils with this man's scent every night until he closed his eyes for the last time.

He woke alone in the bed next morning, but Jimmy made a lump in the other bed. They'd learned the hard way that to make a bed looked slept in, someone must sleep in it, not just toss about for a few minutes. After finding small but important objects, like Jimmy's straight razor with the Bakelite handle, made into the hastily rumpled bed, they gave up the pleasure of holding each other all night for the necessity of allaying Mrs. Deegan's mind.

They dressed, letting Donal retrieve the thought that had bothered him so last night. "What made ye think to go a-sailing on the sea?"

"Politics, what else?" Jimmy shrugged into his tweed jacket, which had acquired a new scorch mark since Donal last looked closely. "I shape metals, I bend tubing, and someone thinks that a man who works with high pressure steam can do the same little trick with exploding gunpowder."

"That's not nearly the same! Does someone want ye to make guns?" Donal stopped short with one boot on.

"Repair them. So far," Jimmy reassured him with a finger drawn along a jawline, "I've been able to say no, 'tis not my skill, I haven't the right tools. But someday soon, someone with shootin' on the mind will realize that a cold boiler, in need of repair, makes an excellent place to store shipments that I do not wish to know about, much less touch, and will ask me to pass such things on. Who do I betray then?"

Never imagining marine boilers becoming a route to armed insurrection, Donal let the other boot fall to the floor.

"I haven't much family to threaten, just my uncle and a sister they may not know about. The rest are dead or emigrated." Jimmy looked into some hideous future in the middle distance, his eyes unfocused over Donal's head. "But if they offer threat to you, Donal—" He snapped back into the here and now. "—I will do anything they want."

That admission catapulted Donal into his Jimmy's arms—he never wanted to let go, if leaving their sanctuary would bring those kinds of choices. But they could not stay here forever—nor could they leave the room red and rumpled. If Jimmy trusted Donal to solve problems he knew about—now he knew. "Fare to America is just under eight pounds in third class. I have a bit put by; I could save the rest in a few months, but we'd need money for two..." He could ask Kitty—she might have saved up almost that much with her new position, but she needed that money for her married life. He could not ask her to delay yet longer for him—she and her man thought they could marry this summer. The *gombeenmen* would ask more interest for a borrower leaving the city.... His calculations carried them out onto the street into the winter dawn.

"No need of that, Donal." Jimmy made sure to walk at a respectable distance—there were other workmen on the sidewalk with them. "Harland and Wolff will deliver twelve ships this year alone. The two tenders are only going as far as Cherbourg, but the others will be sailing to all seven of the seas. That gives me ten ships to try, and time to discover what I need to know of what lies on the other side of the oceans. Perhaps two months."

"That long?" That shook Donal out of his figures.

"Sure—I mean to be on the guarantee crew for one of our fine vessels, and one is destined for the Australia run. I'll go, look, and return, and we'll decide what happens next, and best of all, they'll pay me to do it." Jimmy appeared oblivious to the sour looks from the other men boarding the east-bound tram. His attention was fixed on the huge ship standing dark against the smudge of brightness at the horizon. "Look at her, Donal, the Pride of Belfast—why should I not sail on her?"

"Why don't we all sail away?" grumbled one of the other men, his breath a white plume.

Donal told himself that Jimmy would be coming back if he did go.

Chapter Four

"They've passed me over for an apprentice!" Jimmy stormed. "A bloody apprentice!" He paced the tiny parlor, occasionally stopping long enough to shake a fist at the unkind world. Mrs. Deegan had tried to shush him for language, but his wrath had convinced her something needed stirring in the kitchen, and only Donal remained to hear the rage.

"Alfy fucking Cunningham is going, and I am not." The tempest blew itself out at last—Jimmy collapsed at the table, leaning his face into his hands. Glad that Mrs. Deegan wasn't there to either hear the coarseness or to see him comfort Jimmy with a gripping stroke to one shoulder; Donal tried to console him, and did not mention that an apprentice from his own wood shop was also on the guarantee group.

"The Royal Mail Steam Packet Company will be taking three ships in the next four months, and the Hamburg Teutonic Line, one, Jimmy—does it have to be this one?"

Jimmy looked up with one eye. "Do you recall what we'd talked about back in January?" Donal nodded. "It's started. I said no, and the bastard said, 'It'll be "yes" soon enough; we'll be watching ye.' So yes, it does have to be this ship—I cannot risk ye."

If anyone cared to watch closely, their secret would be out, and there would be danger from more than one quarter. Donal thought to his savings—if Kitty would lend him fifteen shillings, that would be one fare, and Jimmy was a thrifty man....

Abruptly Jimmy was on his feet again, grabbing his cap off the hook by the front door. "I have another thought. I'll be back."

He was, about three hours later, long after the sun had gone down, the dampness of March clinging to his cheeks. "I've done it, Donal, I'm in." He didn't sound nearly so happy to be part of the guarantee group as he had been enraged to be excluded, but Donal couldn't ask why in front of the Deegans, not with that look in his lover's eye.

When they were upstairs behind the closed door, Donal dared to question.

"I'm not part of the guarantee group, precisely. I am, but the group is full, so in another way, I am not. I will have the responsibilities to the ship, but the title and the daily work of a trimmer. But I am going, and it will buy us a month or more before we need to emigrate, and perhaps we'll no longer need to—they'll have made some mistake and been arrested."

"That's good, but... ye aren't pleased." There was something more to it than the prospect of backbreaking work in the bowels of the ship.

"I said once I would do anything to keep ye safe. Shoveling coal is nothing." Jimmy doused the light and came to stand small in Donal's arms. "Don't ask me more."

They slept in the same bed that night, tousled covers be damned, because Jimmy refused to let go, and Donal did not want him to.

***

SEA TRIALS were to begin tomorrow, and the big liner still hummed with unfinished work. The wind had kicked up around noon, howling through the lines, swaying the lifeboats in their davits, and swinging the boxes being lifted aboard at the crane deck. Tugs had pulled the big floating crane away from the deep-water fitting out dock, for fear it would topple in the gale. The crane had lifted entire funnel assemblies and tons of other materiel aboard, but was a danger to the ship now. The smaller, ship-mounted cranes would have to do the lifting, and were only a danger to the men unloading them.

Donal had been working alone, installing woodwork in second class cabins, and there were other cabins yet undone, the porcelain basins still in crates. He stood to stretch, wondering when he could reasonably expect to put down his tools, and whether or not he'd be completing his task tomorrow in the middle of the Irish Sea. The wind beat fitfully at the portholes—if it didn't die down and he had to continue his installations during the sea trials, Donal might become the very first person to be seasick on this ship.

The corridors had rumbled with the passing of a thousand feet some time ago; most of the workers had left at the correct time. It had to be long past five-thirty—Donal's belly complained that Mrs. Deegan wouldn't hold his meal indefinitely, though she knew he would be kept late tonight. One more cabinet bolted to the bulkhead, and then he would trudge home. If they expected him to get another five done tonight, they should have assigned him an apprentice to help. With his pockets full of tools, Donal checked the adjacent cabin, where yet another washstand waited to be

39

attached securely. He stuck his head in and located the drill holes, which, of course, did not line up properly with the bulkhead. He cursed mildly for having this same nuisance with every piece, and shoved the washstand a fraction of an inch to the left. Which, of course, turned out to be a slight fraction too far.

"There you are!" and a pinch on his bum startled Donal into gouging the wood and bashing his head.

"Don't creep up on a man half inside a cupboard!" Donal backed out, half delighted to see Jimmy and half vexed for the surprise. "And what if that had not been my backside ye'd just pinched?"

"I'd know that bum anywhere." Jimmy kissed him and patted the offended cheek. "Though for all it should call to me as the north calls the geese in the spring, I had the devil of a time finding ye. I had to ask two different painters and was nearly squashed flat by some mattresses."

"How peculiar—you generally squash the mattresses." With the door closed, Donal felt brave enough to make the jest.

"I was wandering about, trying to find 'C Deck aft' where the painters both thought ye'd be, and ended up following the men pushing the violent bedding." Jimmy stopped nuzzling Donal to look about the cabin, which had bedsteads but no mattresses. "She doesn't look ready to sail."

"She's ready to sail. She's not entirely ready for passengers, but there's tomorrow and another week at dock before the maiden voyage."

Third class was generally ready, being much plainer; no one from the cabinetry shop had been sent to install anything there, and first class was nearly perfect. Donal had worked on fourteen of the forty-odd ships built in the yard since he started his apprenticeship—this last minute rush to completion was nothing new to him. But Jimmy, whose work had been installed far below almost a year ago, might never have seen the upper decks of this ship or any.

"How does anyone find their way on this great island?" Jimmy wanted to know. He left off hugging Donal to peer out the porthole, leaning enough to tempt Donal into pinching his arse back, even if the next dolly-load of mattresses might come through that door at any moment. Jimmy straightened with a little yelp; the two sacks he carried, one large, one small, bounced off his hip.

"More to the point, why are you up here?" The guard at the gangway turned back everyone who did not have active business, and while Jimmy did have responsibilities, they were several decks below.

"I did not have to shovel—we're banking the furnaces 'til morning. We haven't enough coal to keep her at full boil all night if we aren't sailing in the morning, and the weather is so dicey that Lord Pirrie himself has declared sea trials postponed a day. I shall have to look lively in the morning, but tonight is my own."

They'd loved each other tender goodbyes the night before, not knowing if they'd see each other again in the bustle—these embraces were treasure. Donal ran his hands beneath Jimmy's jacket, one foot braced against the door, and wondered how to get the best use of the time. Tending his belly was not nearly so appealing as the soft whiskery kisses Jimmy was brushing against his neck.

"Shall we go home then?" The travel would take so much time.

41

"I've been home and back, and made your apologies—Mrs. Deegan does not expect us tonight; she believes you are sleeping aboard for an early start in the morning, and I was supposed to be sleeping on board anyway—my first shift with a shovel begins somewhere in the Irish Sea." He grinned wickedly. "But not tomorrow. I'll supervise the early power up as I did today, before assuming my duties in keeping the ship upright."

Loving this man ever harder for taking on the filthy job of moving coal, which did indeed keep the ship from assuming a list, Donal thought he might take Jimmy out for a bite and a jar, before taking him home for a last tumble. Unless they really could sleep aboard...

"Are you finished here? And are you hungry?"

"No, more's the pity, I have this to finish and four more yet, and yes, I'm famished."

Jimmy had the solutions to both in his hands. "I could help." The novelty of working with wood did not explain that big grin, although the packet of sandwiches he offered was something worth grinning for. Donal wolfed them down, glad to be taking him up on both offers. With Jimmy to steady and Donal to drive screws, he could finish much faster.

"You make very pretty washstands," Jimmy observed, and with the help, Donal got four cabins done in the time he'd needed for two before, and there were only twelve to do tomorrow, though the fitters might or might not get the water lines connected before they reached Southampton.

"These are not my prettiest." Mahogany, they were, and polished to a high gloss, but the curlicues around the oval mirrors did not compare to the work he'd done for the priciest suites.

"Show me?"

Weighing the probability of being intercepted, Donal decided to take the risk, sharing his tools into Jimmy's pockets. "Look like we have business and we shouldn't be questioned." He led Jimmy up a staircase to the next deck, down a dimly lit corridor, meeting no one, to a door marked B60. When he stopped, Jimmy ran into him, his eyes on the deck.

"This is very squashy carpet," Jimmy apologized. It was unlike anything they lived with, certainly.

"Then prepare to gawp." Donal led him into the parlor suite, one of the biggest aboard. The electric lights came on at the touch of a switch, unlike the temperamental gas-lights at home, and Jimmy gasped.

"So this is how the quality lives." Wide-eyed, Jimmy roamed through the cabin, the one room with its double bed and parlor sitting area larger than the entire combined first floor at home. He stroked his knuckles against the flocked medallions of the wallpaper, examined the electric lights with their milky glass globes, and tested the spring of the sofa but didn't try sitting. The width of the bed kept his attention for several minutes, and then he found the open doorway to the lavatory. "Is this what I think it is?"

"Amazing about the posh plumbing." Donal pushed a handle, causing a swirling and a roar, and Jimmy to jump backwards. "Self-filling and self-draining tub too."

Jimmy took another gander around him, his reflection in the enormous mirror wide-eyed. "Which did you make?"

"The dressing stand is the only piece for this cabin." Donal pulled out a drawer to show Jimmy the lettering burned into the wood. The shipbuilder's name and address, and his own name, D. Gallagher, below.

"Beautiful." Jimmy ran a finger over the grain of the wood. "Ye have reason to be proud. My work is fine, but not so lovely."

"Indispensable, though. These suites are complete and furnished—no one has reason to come up here, unlike C Deck." Donal turned down the lights, locked the door, and threw cushions from the sofa down in front of the door, lest light leak under it. "Your boilers are lit, there's hot water running. Let's have a fine wash, shall we?"

"Because?" Jimmy paused with his hands on his jacket lapels.

If Jimmy could be bold, then so could Donal. Taking a deep breath, he said, "Because you're leaving for a month and I mean to bid ye safe journey in a millionaire's bed."

"Oh, ye do?" All smiles and growing more bare by the second, Jimmy asked the terrible question. "And if we're caught?"

All his life Donal had been predictable. Good, steady, Donal. Today he'd throw that out the window. "Then I'll borrow fifteen shillings from Kitty and sail along in steerage."

"Oh, Donal, I do love ye." Jimmy dropped his jacket on the floor and caught Donal up in a back-cracking hug. "What does the quality wash with?"

Peeling a cake of soap, careful to not tear the picture of the ship on the wrapper, Donal sniffed deeply. "Vinolia should get our sweaty carcasses clean." Jimmy tucked the flattened wrapper into his pocket. A man who had not been allowed to watch this ship launch, he must want the souvenir. Donal turned on the tap, flinching at the sound of the water and testing it for temperature. It ran hot in a few minutes, and any engineers below should attribute the flow to the fitters testing the connections in Donal's wake. Jimmy tested the contents of the bottle from the little rack, rubbing his fingers together with a thoughtful look while they waited for the warm water. "Contra-Mar Beauty Fluid" said the label with the pretty girl in traveling clothes.

Kneeling together in the tub and careful not to splash, Donal and Jimmy ran soap-slick hands over one another, trading kisses and scrubbing. Not since he was a child had anyone bathed him—Donal liked the custom now, and ventured his sudsy way around Jimmy. Slick bellies pressed together, foamy with more bubbles than any cake of soap Donal had ever met could produce. Jimmy swept the flannel up and down Donal's back, the slight scratchiness almost as good as a kiss, but he didn't have to have one or the other—he took both, the day's whiskers around his mouth catching at Jimmy's stubble.

"Shall I shave for ye, *mo stór?* The razor's in me bag." Jimmy was already leaning half out of the tub to find that treasure, a gift from his late father for making journeyman. "We can shave you too."

Smooth chins were for early morning embraces and Saturday nights. Donal worked up a handful of lather for Jimmy's cheeks, feeling the rasp of the softening whiskers against his palms. Jimmy closed his eyes, swaying slightly with the caresses and puffing a bit of foam away from his mouth. His beard was heavier than Donal's, the reddish tint showing against the pale skin, though it blended with the freckles that dusted Jimmy's cheeks. He'd experimented with a mustache as so many of the other workmen wore, but gave it up after leaving a red mark on Donal's fair neck.

Jimmy stroked with the straight blade, honed to an edge meant to last the voyage, across his cheek. Donal did nothing to distract him, glad that shelter of the channel kept the ship from tossing in the wind. Out on the open sea, he would not let Jimmy risk his throat.

"And you."

Donal tightened his upper lip, the only spot that grew more than a few silky blond hairs, feeling, but not watching, Jimmy slide the wicked blade over his skin. He did a brief pass over cheeks and neck, with Donal trusting his Adam's apple to Jimmy's skill. Their love was a different kind of blade to each other's necks, but Donal trusted Jimmy not to nick him that way either.

Clean now, but enjoying the bath too much to leave it, Donal rinsed his face in fresh running water, turned on just for the moment, such a luxury. Soaping his hands again, he went back to caressing Jimmy, whose round arse he'd never explored wet.

Their baths in the kitchen at home were solitary affairs by necessity, and Donal had only seen Jimmy fully naked and wet once before. During their holiday week the previous summer, they'd gone tramping in the hills past Ballygomartin and come upon an old quarry, filled with water that still held a chill. They were not the only ones to find it—the quarry rang with laughter and splashes from the score of other men who'd gotten there first. Clothing hung on bushes everywhere, for not a stitch had gone into the water with the bathers. Jimmy and Donal hesitated only a moment before stripping down, leaping in, and discovering Jimmy couldn't swim.

In the warm water and privacy, Donal could reach out for more than a rescue. Jimmy's butt would be most amazingly clean, what with both of Donal's soapy hands travelling over his cheeks, bringing the fine hairs lined up in the suds, and one hand slipping between. Drawing the length of his finger along Jimmy's hole, he could feel the little ridges jumping with each pass. He teased Jimmy, playing at the entrance to bring those little sharp breaths Donal loved, the ones that threatened to become little yelps of excitement.

"Do that more," Jimmy begged in the soft voice they'd trained themselves to use, though he could have spoken more loudly tonight. Swiveling around until his back pressed to Donal's chest, he straddled Donal's knee and pulled one of Donal's hands to his groin.

The water lapped around their thighs while Donal continued his foamy exploration between Jimmy's cheeks, sometimes halting the long sweeps to tickle lightly at Jimmy's hole and hear him moan. He could reach Jimmy's groin, too, and with one hand to encircle Jimmy's cock, he could slither across the private places and still slide his tongue across Jimmy's back. Reaching lower, Donal cupped Jimmy's balls, drawn tight against his body now, then took long, slow pulls at his cock. Jimmy groaned low in his throat and went taut, pulsing against Donal's hands.

"Ye could have gone in." Jimmy at last caught his breath. "'Tis a narrow passage, but we were slick."

"Soap burns," Donal murmured. He'd tried it once, alone in the galvanized tub. "I didn't want t' spoil your moment." He would have liked to go in. Perhaps the posh soap would be nicer than what they had at home, but he wouldn't risk this wonderful night on being wrong.

"Ah. I've only tried it wet." Jimmy twisted again, facing Donal and meeting his mouth. "We'll try you wet?"

Donal didn't think his cock could get any harder, until Jimmy said that, followed by "Lie back, *mo ghrá;* I need to see ye."

His cock throbbed against his belly, the water splashing up to lick the droplets oozing from the tip. Jimmy lifted one of Donal's legs, resting his ankle on a shoulder; Donal placed his other leg up unasked. Jimmy pressed his lips to Donal's skin.

"Ye're a fair sight." He rubbed his cheek on Donal's other shin, running his hands up Donal's thighs. "I could look at ye forever."

"I'll look back." Jimmy, his skin glistening with the wetness, the little patch of hair at his breastbone lying flat to his pale skin, his face so open and soft, was a more than fair sight; he was a beloved sight, framed there between Donal's knees.

Both hands soapy, Jimmy cradled Donal's cock, swirling his hands over shaft and balls, turning them white with lather, making the dark blond hair and purplish head stand out where they peeked through. Shuddering made waves to slap his skin; lifting his hips to thrust into Jimmy's hands made tides. As Donal had done, Jimmy now did, moving between Donal's cheeks to caress and play, never stopping the slow pumping at his cock, only Jimmy chased the suds away before Donal could no longer keep from begging him to come in.

The splashing lifted his balls, dancing them in the water, making Donal close his eyes. He wanted to watch Jimmy's face when he entered, but every nerve was tuned below, where fingertips stroked, spread, and stole in. One searching finger broached him, sliding in sweetly, then out again, to the rhythm of Jimmy's encircling hand. His grip on Jimmy's thighs was no longer enough—Donal drew Jimmy forward with pressure from his legs, supporting him, yet wordlessly demanding. Opening ever wider to his lover, Donal turned the kiss from sweet to fiery with his tongue.

"Oh, Jimmy," he gasped out, the words pushed from him. "I love ye so."

"And I love ye, Donal." Jimmy stilled everywhere, hands, mouth, even his breath, before going on again. "I will come back to ye, I swear it."

He'd made that promise last night too, but Donal near wept to hear it again. "See that ye do, for I need ye." He brushed his mouth against Jimmy's again. "I need to look at ye."

Jimmy rose up again, easing the fold in Donal's middle and doing something especially wondrous with one hand. "Is this good?"

"Oh, very good!" What had Jimmy touched inside? Could he do more of it?

Jimmy looked down at his hands, working their magic on Donal's body."Do I dare two fingers?" One finger was all they'd ever tried, or even talked about.

"We can try." Donal opened one eye, looking at Jimmy's hand, then at his half-mast cock, thinking, and spread his knees a bit farther.

"I'll stop if ye say." Jimmy twiddled his fingers mid-air, his long middle finger pressed first to one companion, then the other. He pursed his lips, examining three together for an instant, but flared his hand wide and came back to two when Donal grunted with a bit more alarm than he'd intended. He hadn't meant to make a noise, but really, first things first.

"We don't have to do this," Jimmy pointed out.

Donal tried to believe that Jimmy's hands had not suddenly expanded to three times their usual size. They were just hands, a bit work-scarred, but the same hands that had caressed him to ecstasy every night for months. "But we can."

Leaning in, Jimmy kissed him softly—Donal took it as a promise for the touch. Jimmy's fingers went back to their proper size.

Jimmy's other hand hadn't stopped its up and down motion, only slowed as they talked. Donal focused on that, nonetheless feeling Jimmy fumbling at his backside, trying to work a second finger in. He pulled out completely—what he did with his other thumb wasn't enough of a distraction to keep Donal from noticin'— and returned, successful, from the burn of it. A small mewl came out, to his concern, for Jimmy stopped.

"Is this...?"

A nod, for a word couldn't come out, though from the surprise or the feel, Donal didn't know.

Jimmy pushed in a little farther. "It's very tight. And I don't think the water's helping." He withdrew an inch and returned, slowly, and his other hand stopped. "Ye're not enjoying this."

"It's new. Keep on." But Donal knew why Jimmy said that—his cock had drooped, even though Jimmy's hand had traveled his length, pulling the skin over 'til the head disappeared and then poked out again.

"Ye're not enjoying it." He removed both hands and found the soap. "Even if it's new, and ye might come to like it better, it will wait; I don't want to take the memory of your face pinched up away with me. Time enough to find out when I return." Jimmy pulled Donal to sitting, his backside making it clear that what they'd done needed something more than they had so far. "Even without the posh plumbing." It didn't matter so much, wrapped in Jimmy's arms. There would be time.

"Can you imagine doing this at home in the kitchen?" Donal murmured, lifting Jimmy to his feet to wrap in a towel.

The water swirled around their ankles in its leaving instead of getting thrown on the back garden. Donal could not, nor could he imagine what their loving would be like on a sprung mattress, but he intended to find out, and he led Jimmy out to more luxury.

They tucked themselves under the deep blue satin coverlet, Donal's hair damp on an amazingly fluffy pillow, Jimmy's head on his shoulder. He'd nearly gotten maudlin last night—a body'd think Jimmy was emigrating alone with an insincere promise of sending for him, instead of moving heaven and earth to get a round trip with a pay packet to bring home. Tonight he could hold Jimmy quietly and make the memory of it last.

"It will only be a month, if that—we set sail from New York on the twentieth, and will get passage back from

51

Portsmouth." Jimmy murmured, as if reading Donal's mind. "Ye'll have enough to keep ye busy enough not to miss me."

"If I have to complete every scrap of woodwork on the *Deseado* alone, I will miss you, Jimmy." He drew a finger across Jimmy's newly shaven cheek. "You with your twenty-three bunkmates, now..."

"That will be twenty-three I don't want—there's only one I do." Jimmy pulled up to gaze down at Donal. They hadn't doused the small electric lamp, but Donal didn't need to see Jimmy's face to know the sincerity. He'd look into those blue eyes forever. He pulled Jimmy down for a kiss that started softly, and grew.

They rolled together in a tangle of arms, legs, and hungry mouths, squirming together amid squeaks far louder than their beds at home. It didn't matter—no one had reason to be on this deck, no one would wonder about the dim light through the window seen from the far shore of the River Lagan, no one could come through that door without a key. Donal tried to inhale Jimmy, to consume him, to melt into him, and from underneath, Jimmy bucked back to him, as if they could meld their very selves.

Sliding over one another again, Donal had to take great desperate handfuls of Jimmy, gripping 'round an upper arm, cupping a warm handful of butt, feeling the strength in his thigh. Gentle with Jimmy's groin, Donal still had to roll the stones within his sack, finally wrapping his fingers around Jimmy's shaft, hard again, needy and soon to be out of reach. For now Donal could grasp him, rub the soft skin over the hard column within, and still plunge his tongue into Jimmy's willing mouth.

Thirty nights' of kisses they tried to take all at once, thirty nights' of skin pressing to skin, and unknown years of rolling in a bed wide enough to keep them from falling off. Jimmy spurted between them, slowing Donal enough to honor the climax.

"Now you," Jimmy whispered, sliding down Donal's body, pausing to lick his own fluid from Donal's belly, then kissing lower. "I'm glad I didn't spoil the flavor."

Donal stopped wondering what that meant—Jimmy sucked every thought from his head, sliding so far down his shaft that Donal could feel breath in his curls, then coming back up with deliberation that turned to abandon. Then he was lost in the dazzle of his climax—no man who would sail in this cabin could be richer than he, with Jimmy's lips wrapped around him.

They were tired, true, but they were young—Donal woke with Jimmy snug behind him. He twined his fingers into Jimmy's', lifting his hand for a brief brush of lips across battered workman's knuckles, amazed at waking together. He felt lips move at the back of his neck—good, Jimmy was awake, too.

"If I had a million pounds I would live like this." Donal wiggled back against Jimmy. "Luxurious beds and you in them, and the world could *pogue ma thoin.*"

"You have me in your bed, and I don't want the world kissing that—it's mine to play with." Jimmy shoved his hips hard against the as-yet-unkissed section. "I have a thought, don't move." Much stretching and grunting, then Jimmy produced the bottle from the bathroom. "Give us a hand."

Working together, they got the bottle uncapped and a dollop of the contents into Jimmy's palm. Donal jumped forward away from the chill when Jimmy reached between them, but only a dab went on him—Jimmy groaned with the movement of his hand. "Now some for you."

The lotion was nice, even if it smelled of something flowery, and with Jimmy's hand working him up and down that way, and Jimmy's cock, all hard again, slipping between his bum cheeks. The goo was more slippery than anything they'd had, except for the one time they'd dared steal a lump of butter from the kitchen. Mrs. Deegan had noticed the theft.

Jimmy rocked against him from behind, as if they'd never fallen asleep, his cock sliding in the trough of Donal's bum, his free hand working Donal's hard cock. As nice as it felt, Jimmy kept losing the rhythm, or his hand slid off completely from this peculiar slick lotion. Donal rolled to his belly to hump the mattress while Jimmy humped him, and it would all be fine except— He hadn't counted on this unfamiliar oil and now— "Jimmy, hold!"

Jimmy froze—was this as strange for him as for Donal? Breathing shallowly, Donal tried to decide if what had happened was good or bad, if he should ask Jimmy to back away—or come closer.

"Am I hurting ye?"

"Wait!" He didn't want to say "yes" too soon—the startle might be the worst part. "It's easing. Just—wait." He took more deep breaths.

The feeling was different than two fingers in the tub, but they hadn't had this Contra-Mar lotion to ease the way, and the pressure wasn't the same. Donal sucked more air in, remembering the twenty tons of soap and tallow that had glided this behemoth ship from gantry to water. That voyage was far more improbable than Jimmy's cock suddenly poking into his arse, and he decided this was as much of a one way journey. He could feel Jimmy trembling against his back, and suddenly feared Jimmy might go soft. "Is it too tight for ye?"

"No. Oh, Donal— " Jimmy stopped talking, brushing his lips across Donal's neck instead.

"Come in." Spreading his thighs for Jimmy, Donal flexed, relaxed, and pushed, suddenly finding the way to welcome him. "That's good, yes— Ah!"

Jimmy froze again, and Donal hadn't the breath to tell him that meant *good*. Instead, he lifted his hips until Jimmy was once more pressed firmly against his bum, letting the fullness and stretch go from odd to right. "Take me slow."

Slow, oh yes, Jimmy took him slow, stopping once to add a bit more grease. Like an engine worked in, Donal thought he could go faster, and Jimmy matched him, bringing small starbursts with his thrusts, his hands tight on Donal's shoulders and his breath hot on Donal's cheek. When he spent, Donal felt the pulses as never before, pushing the orgasms through them both with this new connection, and the sharing blanked his mind.

Jimmy's voice was a worried buzz in his ear before he made sense of the words. "Did ye like that? I didn't plan to—I didn't mean to—Donal, love, did I hurt ye?"

"Shush, *mo mhíle stór, shush*." He tried to turn—Jimmy let him roll over and snuggle tight. "Had I known ship's stores had a potion to let us do this, we'd have booked passage long ago."

***

DONAL HAD NEVER expected to travel on this ship, and he wasn't enjoying it now, even though his Jimmy was three decks below, working diligently. Some cack-handed hauler had bashed a piece of furniture into a second-class staircase, and if sea trials hadn't been postponed a day, his quickly-lathed uprights would have been sent to Southampton and installed there. Instead, he and another joiner had pried off the banister—this ship would be as perfect as they could make her.

They and the woodwork had left the Belfast Lough that morning—the high winds had died down enough to let the tugs pull the ship down the River Lagan, into the lough, then turned her loose to the sea. Donal had worked through the maneuvers until the emergency stop—unannounced, but he should have expected it. The ship fought the sea for half a mile, nearly bringing his dinner back before she halted. He wondered how Jimmy was faring down in the bowels of the ship, where he fed the insatiable furnaces.

Tasks as completed as they could be, Donal and a few other workers sailed back to Belfast in the splendor of the engineers' mess, though others worked through the day and would continue to paint and unpack all the way to Southampton. They disembarked to roars from the crowd gathered at the dock.

He and Jimmy had said their farewells that night in B60—Donal could still feel part of them in his backside, and the rest of the magic bottle lay secreted in the wardrobe, waiting for Jimmy's return. Now he joined the dockside crowd. All of Belfast had gathered on the banks of the river.

Not quite an hour passed before the tugs roared once again into the evening, laboring to bring their charge away into the channel. Like tiny terriers straining at their leashes, leading their mistress where they wished to go, the tugs pulled the ship away from the dock, escorting her back to the Lough and the sea. Someone in the crowd, overcome by the majesty of the moment, began to sing "Rule, Britannia," and voices joined in, up and down the banks.

Donal sang, not caring for missed notes; the few sounds he could make came through his nearly closed throat. This ship they had labored over for three years was bearing his love away—the tears blurring his vision did not care that Jimmy would be back in a month's time, full of plans. One droplet ran down his cheek and fell to the ground, perhaps trying to reach the water to help float Jimmy safe. The rest turned the ship to a great black ghost with a white smudge at the stern that read *Titanic*.

Chapter Five

"FOUR HOURS ON, eight hours off, do it all again," the leading fireman informed Jimmy. "Here's your new best mate." The long shovel wasn't a good patch on Donal, but Jimmy figured he'd become just as well acquainted with it by voyage's end.

He'd thrown his few things onto a bunk in the trimmers' bunk room in the prow of the ship on E Deck. Twenty-four bunks in here, nothing to distinguish it much from the bunk room across the corridor or the one that angled to a point just beyond.

"If you don't like the bunk ye've got, just wait until we reach Southampton—most of these lads won't be going farther and ye can grab what ye want before the new hands come in," advised another trimmer, who had snagged the last lower berth.

Jimmy didn't like the upper berth by the door at all, but he'd only be in it one sleep shift, maybe two. "There's one stairs ye're allowed to use to get to the firemen's mess on C Deck. We don't want yer grimy mug scarin' the paying passengers, and there's nowhere else ye need to go that ye can't reach on Scotland Road or the tunnel below on the tank top."

So began his sojourn in Hell: scoop, twist, dump, trundle, dump, return, scoop, twist.... Four hours of work heavier because of the repetition, and Jimmy could only wonder that the other men had breath to sing—after three hours in the inferno he had no mind left to learn the tunes. Six hundred tons of coal this hungry ship would eat each day on the sea, and he would be moving around eight tons of it, one barrow load at a time. It had sounded like a better idea when he'd accepted the position.

The holds weren't near full; the coal strike in Wales meant they'd have to take on what they could get in Southampton, and Jimmy glumly expected to shift it all himself. Scoop, twist, dump....

He'd toiled, eaten, and slept twice when they arrived at Southampton and the trimmers' bunks grew empty. They'd keep two boilers running at dock, to power the ship's electrical lights and machinery. Thousands of pounds of fresh meat, vegetables, eggs, and butter had to be taken on and refrigerated. Jimmy couldn't complain about the food—portions he'd never seen before of foodstuffs that didn't often grace Mrs. Deegan's table—just the amount of jam on the bread made him look twice. Beef and mutton in quantities they didn't see at Christmas appeared on large platters three times a day, and if the crew ate so well, what marvels appeared at table for the passengers in first class? He ate every scrap and still didn't feel well enough fueled to go back into the coal holds.

The dockside work was relatively light, and Jimmy wasn't called upon to fix any of his twenty-nine creations. He even had a chance to go ashore a few times that week. Work on the ship stopped for Easter Sunday, except for the black gang who kept the power running. He did get a bath that day, and suspected it would take more than one to get all the coal dust off his skin. Donal probably wouldn't touch him without a good scouring first—that prissy Vinolia soap in first class wasn't up to the task.

Thoughts of Donal kept him shoveling though his arms and chest burned with the effort. He had not told Donal the half of the story—a ship with contraband was due into the yard for refitting sometime in April. Strangers with hard eyes had told him to be ready to shift bundles he could never talk about. Jimmy did not expect Home Rule to improve the country in any way, but he would not pass along death to keep from finding out.

He would have liked time and privacy to think of Donal. The hero's send-off he'd given Jimmy needed contemplation. He wanted to remember the joy, of course, but he had to think of other things, too—what they'd tried in the bath had brought real winces, but Donal lying under him in the bed had urged him on with words and body. And his face— Jimmy knew what it meant when Donal's face went slack like that. But privacy didn't exist in the parts of the ship permitted to him, though a greaser whispered of a corner in the fireman's lavatory where a man's needs could be met. Jimmy had no use for that: he'd been loved in a parlor suite three decks above.

The colliers came alongside the day after Easter, ready to drop the tons of fuel through the chutes and into the ten coal holds. The trimmers would level it all off, moving it from one hold to the other, or to furnaces, as needed to keep the ship trim, or level.

"Number six hold is too hot," reported a more experienced hand who'd joined the ship there. Jimmy wondered how he could tell—it was all excessively warm to him. "Have we got a bleedin' fire?"

"Start the pumps, and tell the colliers to hold off," the shift boss said. One man bolted for the firemen's stairs, another for the switch. But it was too late—the rumble of the falling coal drowned out the curses at the door to the number six hold.

"Now what?" Jimmy asked, once the noise stopped.

"Put another four hundred gallons on it, and then we'll start shiftin' the bitch." The lead trimmer threw his shovel into the corner with a clang.

"What happened?"

"The coal dries out too far and sets its bitchin' self on fire, and then the shite-eatin' colliers drop another hundred tons on it." The lead trimmer spat a huge black glob against the coal hold door, where it evaporated rather quickly. Perhaps that was a test and he would have worried if it sizzled?

"So what do we do?"

"We, meaning you, laddie, get to drag the good coal into the other bunkers, we drop the burning mass into the furnaces when we can get at it, and we go our merry way. 'Course, we may be halfway across the friggin' Atlantic before it's all out." The lead trimmer's teeth shone white, with a few brown spots, against his dust-blackened skin. "Don't fash yourself, it happens often enough. We'll keep the pumps on it."

Great, bloody great. They hadn't even left the dock of their first port and somehow his beautiful ship, with its hundred-fifty nine furnaces where *well-behaved* coal burned, had managed to set herself afire and no one even suggested telling an officer. Bloody wonderful.

***

THE BEDROOM ECHOED empty without Jimmy—he'd been Donal's *ghrá* for almost a year now, and the lonely times, nearly forgotten, were upon him once more. An evening at the pub brought questions from the other regulars about Jimmy, and the music didn't sound the same without his pennywhistle. The newspapers were small consolation for company: the headlines were never cheerful and the dates ticked off too slowly.

Jimmy must be enjoying himself in Southampton. Nearly a week at dock for supply and final fitting would leave a coal trimmer with little to do, though if he had to repair any malfunctions in the steam pipes, he might be the busiest man on ship. Donal rather hoped Jimmy was loafing about—holidays were hard come by, with only a week off in the summer and a few days around religious festivals. Donal spent his two days off at Easter, which fell exactly a week after Jimmy sailed, making plans for their Christmas, for surely they'd be together. He had a great many ideas that might be possible only in America.

April tenth—Jimmy would be leaving Southampton, though he'd have started shoveling in earnest twenty-four hours earlier to get the boilers to sailing pressure. He'd make a brief stop in Cherbourg to pick up the passengers coming from Paris. On the eleventh, he, and of course the ship, would touch at Queenstown, and that's the last Jimmy would see of Ireland for weeks. The guarantee group would leave the *Titanic* in Portsmouth, take ship to Belfast, and that would bring Jimmy back to him, perhaps as early as the twenty-seventh. He could wait that long, he told himself, and he shouldn't worry, for wasn't his love aboard the finest ship on the ocean?

April fifteenth—Jimmy must be nearly to America now. Donal was almost used to the thought of him being on a voyage, now that the month was half over, though he wasn't looking forward to another quiet evening with only the prospect of losing another game of chess to Mr. Deegan. The ructions outside the dockyards halted the flood of workers leaving—everyone stopped to buy papers from the ten and twelve-year-old boys yelling, "*Titanic* hits iceberg! *Virginian* towing to Halifax!"

Amid grumblings of "What have they done with our ship?" and "How will they get her back here from Halifax?" Donal dropped his ha'penny into the boy's hand and darted away to find out what had happened. He nearly stumbled over a bale of newsprint and a different shouting newsboy with grimmer tidings. "*Titanic* rams berg! Ship sunk! All hands saved!"

Grabbing one of those papers too, Donal clutched the contradictory reports, desperate to get out of the throng and find out what had happened—whose news was fresher? More accurate? Six newspapers that seldom agreed with one another had all brought cartloads of papers and boys to hawk them, and all screaming different degrees of calamity. "*Titanic* sunk with all hands!" blared one headline, and the boy didn't yell his wares for the weeping, but only waved the papers and took the money. That paper was not known for commitment to the truth—Donal hoped the boy was crying because the agent driving the cart had clouted his ear for the effect. He bought a copy anyway.

He peeked at headlines and couldn't unfurl any one paper enough to read on the tram, but the talk was all "how could this happen?" Had their beautiful ship failed all her passengers or were the papers only screeching for the sales? Donal tried to shut his ears against the speculations that the worst had really happened. Once home, he tore into the papers, Mrs. Deegan clucking over his shoulder.

"This all means 'no one really knows,' Donal," she tried to comfort him, but her eyes said, 'something bad has happened.' "They'll have real news tomorrow."

The next day was worse—he'd lain awake praying, and every time he drifted off, he dreamed of Jimmy in the cold Atlantic. His Jimmy, who had gone to protect Donal, sank with the ship, or worse, a dozen times. Swimming at the quarry, Donal had reached out to retrieve a man who was only surprised—all night Jimmy screamed into icy waters, their hands turning liquid, passing through one another.

No one at the shop was unaffected, and the foreman didn't press them. Young William Campbell, joiner's apprentice, had been part of the guarantee group. When all were imagining the fate of one of their own, Donal had two to grieve.

The papers—unanimous at last – claimed the ship had gone down. All were saved—some were saved—the *Virginian* became the *Carpathia* and the death toll leaped out from every headline as a different number. Names didn't start appearing in the papers and on the large sign the Harland and Wolff management put up outside the drafting office doors until the eighteenth—the *Carpathia* had arrived in New York with survivors. Donal didn't recall the last time he'd eaten and couldn't bear to sleep—*where was Jimmy?* At meal breaks he'd run to the drafting office to fight his way through the other men searching for answers, and come away churning for not knowing. None of the guarantee group's names appeared in the survivors' lists, no matter how hard he looked. Nor did Jimmy's name appear in the lists of known dead.

He saw Jimmy everywhere from the corner of his eye—any man with a cap the same shade of brown or a jacket the right gray-green tweed gave him hope. Hundreds of Jimmies turned back to the riveters or framers they were, but not before jerking his heart from his chest.

Donal was not the only one looking for Jimmy.

Sitting at table Friday night for yet another supper he would barely touch, Donal jerked around at the thumping. Someone knocked at the door as if he bore it a personal grudge. Donal decided he was best suited to answer—little Mr. Deegan had never overpowered anything with more fight in it than a pint.

"Easy on the door, friends," he told the three men on the stoop. Dressed as everyone else did at the yard, with flat caps, woolen jackets, the color of the wooly jumper the only variation, Donal couldn't say he recognized these men, though they looked back at him with a knowing air that chilled him through.

"We're friends of Jimmy Healy," one announced, though friendliness did not live on his face. Donal already knew it for a lie—in nearly a year, he'd met everyone whose company Jimmy liked enough to seek out. Outright threat—not yet, but this man was serious about his business.

"Aye, we'd like him to join us at the pub," another volunteered. "Ye can come too, if ye like."

Donal would go nowhere with these men that he was not dragged—if Jimmy had feared such men so much that he'd finagled his way aboard the ship, Donal would not waste his sacrifice.

"I'll not be joining ye, thanks all the same." He could not let that statement hang unsupported—these men might not be ready to offer violence outright, but their stiffened backs said they could change their minds, and soon. "This is a house of mourning, ye see."

"Our condolences, and who was it that ye lost?" The leader looked confused, and well he might, for none of the traditional signs hung upon the door.

"We cannot be sure, for there is hope yet—" Donal spoke through the leaden certainty that his Jimmy was not coming home. "But Jimmy was aboard the—" He had not said the words aloud, and to say it to these men put knives into his heart. "—the *Titanic*."

"He was?" Confusion replaced the determination in their faces.

"He was part of the guarantee group." That much Donal could get out without choking. "None of them have been among the living so far." Jimmy had not been listed among the dead, either—Donal could hope, oh, did he hope. But these men needed to believe that Jimmy was beyond their reach.

"A great shame," said one, and the others murmured assent, the aggression falling away, softening their stances. "Again, our condolences."

It hurt to thank these men, knowing why they'd come, but Donal could give no sign that he suspected them of anything but a friendly visit. When at last he'd shut the door on them, he watched through the parlor window, seeing the future in a way that Jimmy must have seen, where everyone took sides, however unwilling.

These men or others like them would not come back to their door, for now. Wondering what would have become of them both had Jimmy been there, Donal could find only the tiniest of solaces that Jimmy had not been required to do their bidding. His journey across the ocean had given Donal the safety Jimmy had said he would buy at any price, but oh, Donal counted the cost too high.

Mrs. Deegan finally put him to bed with toasted bread and a shot of whiskey.

"It's overdue—the yard will be closed tomorrow. A half day for all the deaths. There will be a service." She sat by Donal's side and got the toast into him by sheer force of will. He drank the whiskey more readily—it might dull the pain. "Ye could cry for him, Donal." She stroked his hair, gone lank with neglect, away from his face. "He was your friend and a good man. It will help."

"Have you cried for him, Mrs. Deegan?" The tears, given permission, made his voice hoarse.

"Child, I've lost three little ones, survived *An Gorta Beag,* and buried more than I can count. I have no tears left." She leaned down to kiss his forehead and take the whiskey glass. "But you could cry for him."

He did, lying in Jimmy's bed, wishing it was enough to drown him too.

Chapter Six

"Last chance to go ashore; let's get a drink and a bit of skirt!" His trimmer chum nearly dragged Jimmy out the bunkroom door. "The Grapes will let us in like this."

"Wait!" Jimmy dove after his pennywhistle—his pockets were already loaded with the things he could absolutely not afford to lose. He'd learned the wisdom of keeping his most treasured possessions upon him; he'd found another trimmer rifling his bag the last time he'd gone out. What little coin he'd brought already jingled in his pocket, playing a tune against the handle of his razor, which he'd had to retrieve by force from the would-be thief. The rest of his savings nestled within his featherbed at home—his cushion for the new life he and Donal would start.

Once before they'd followed others of the black gang to a Southampton dock-side pub that tolerated the grime and coal dust stuck to the engine crew. He'd played his whistle then to keep from getting more than the pint he wanted—the tunes had been reason enough not to get cozy with the barmaids, who had second-hand coal dust stuck to them, much of it in the shape of handprints.

Jimmy and his mates been hard at work since yesterday, building up the steam the ship would need to leave the dock, mostly with the coal they were still heaving off the fire. He wouldn't have need to get off during their brief stop at Cherbourg, and the pursers would be especially vigilant at Queenstown, where the steamship lines expected deserters, so this would be the last land under his feet 'til he got to New York. He followed half a dozen chums down the gangway.

Perhaps the third pint wasn't wise, for it made his friend decide that a second trip to the back room with one of the bar girls was a good idea just when someone was teaching a new tune. Jimmy sank into the tune, and didn't think of the time, nor did their companions, who knocked back another and patted the table in time to the music. When the man reemerged from behind the curtain still buttoning his trousers, it was to the sound of a ship's whistle, three long blasts.

"Run, damn ye!"

They ran for all they were worth, if not quite in a straight line, toward the dock. The *Titanic,* in all her immensity, still sat at the dock—they pelted to the crew's gangway at the prow.

"You're late." The purser had already clipped the chain across the door and detached the gangway from the ship. "You've deserted and forfeited your pay."

"We're here, we're in good time!" they begged, but neither Jimmy's silver-tongued pleading nor his companions' curses made a bit of difference. The purser swung the hatch shut.

The seven of them fell silent, boggled that they'd been stranded and that anything they'd left on board would be going to New York without them.

"We could try the passengers' gangway?" Jimmy looked hopefully at the distant ramp.

"If ye wish to be tossed overboard for insolence, sure." That gangway was cast off as they watched. The tugs started to growl, changing pitch from the other side of the ship.

"Fuck, we're marooned." All Jimmy's plotting, planning, and sacrifice to get on that ship had been undone—how would he explain this to Donal? How would he learn what he needed to know to take the two of them out of harm's way? The fine for "boiling can" was nothing compared to this. The cost for that last pint had grown too large to pay.

"Ye great eejit, this is a port." His drinking companion flung his hand at all the black and white ways to leave. "There's a ship, and there's a ship. And, oh goodness gracious, there's a*nother* ship. And more ships tomorrow, and more the day after. How can ye be marooned?"

Right. Of course. He was a fool—he only had to get to America and back, he did not need to do it on one particular vessel. They watched the *Titanic* inch away from the dock and out into the channel of the River Test, where other ships lined the banks. It was rather hypnotic to watch her go and know that someone else was breaking his back to make that happen.

Titanic glided past the docked ships, dwarfing them, ignoring them in her majesty. And then—one ship, perhaps a quarter of her size, began to strain toward the center of the channel, her mooring lines pulling taut, snapping with a *twang* audible from half a mile away.

"On, no, they're going to hit!" The smaller ship's bow swung out into the current made by the leviathan, but no cacophony of stricken plating erupted, and it seemed disaster had been averted.

"The *Olympic* already had a collision," Jimmy mused, and the reports had sounded much like what they'd just watched—a smaller ship drawn into the wake of the larger.

"They're so big. No one really knows how to sail them," opined the trimmer, much sobered by what they'd just witnessed.

"A fire on board and a near miss—I think, somehow, that I am much happier not to be on her." The most sober of Jimmy's drinking companions pointed out the labor agent's office. "Come on, lads, let's find us a ship."

***

THE DAYS TURNED to nights and the nights turned to days of never seeing the sun. The only way Jimmy knew they'd arrived was that the ship stopped moving. Donal's washstands got better looks at New York than he did. Even when they'd arrived, the captain had not let any of them off the ship! No newspapers, no walking about, no meeting people. Were they afraid of desertion? They couldn't know he had the best reason in the world for him to get back in that ship—Donal was waiting for him. But no, not one foot off the ship in the fourteen days since he'd boarded, and the one newspaper that a dockhand smuggled to them had been confiscated by the purser before they'd read more than a headline about "Hearings Begun on Disaster" and the winner of a marathon. Jimmy still didn't know what sort of disaster—what did these Americans get excited about?

Then it was back into the coal holds to shovel his way east.

For all the good his trip to New York had done, Jimmy should have stayed home. No news and his jacket no longer fit, something he hadn't noticed until he'd changed ships in Portsmouth. Belowdecks he hadn't worn more than an undershirt and a pair of trousers that he'd hacked off above the knee—the heat made it impossible to dress in more. The ship had changed but the schedule had not. Four hours on, eight hours off left him exhausted. He'd been fortunate to catch a ship bound for Belfast practically the moment he'd left the *Carmania* in Portsmouth and spent the entire voyage scrubbing and sleeping.

Feeling a bit unsteady on a surface that wasn't pitching and rolling beneath him, Jimmy was perfectly happy not to be a trimmer any longer. On a soft spring day like this—it was May Day, and he wished he could bring Donal a May basket or at least a souvenir of the trip—a man should be walking in the sunshine, not trapped in the guts of a ship. He skipped the tram to stretch his legs, and to save the fare. A trimmer who was just a trimmer did not get paid nearly so well as a trimmer who was part of the guarantee group in some strange unofficial way; he hadn't been able to sign on as an engineer. That was trouble for Monday—he was going to have to explain why he didn't return with the rest. If he and Donal decided they didn't have to emigrate, he'd need to secure his job all over again.

Just now Jimmy didn't want to think one moment beyond the welcome he hoped to get when he walked through the front door—which was not Mrs. Deegan crossing herself, Mr. Deegan dropping his mug of tea, and Donal fainting dead away.

***

The roaring faded from tugboats straining to the tram's hum, though Donal's head throbbed where he'd struck it. A blow could make a man see things, and Jimmy was kneeling over him. Or had Donal cracked his pate so thoroughly that this angel had come to fetch him?

"Am I dead too?" If he was, it hadn't been so bad and here was his Jimmy. That didn't explain Mrs. Deegan and the cold wet cloth she was pressing to his scalp.

"Not for want of trying." Jimmy took over sponging. "But since I'm not dead, what's this "too" business?"

"They never know it, poor dears," Mrs. Deegan whispered and crossed herself again.

"Never know what?" Jimmy inspected for bleeding and put the compress back hard enough to hurt. "I've been to America and back without seeing what I'd gone to see, and now I'm home, only a day later than I'd expected."

"You shouldn't have left Heaven for that, Jimmy." But Donal was glad he had, for this one last look, and the warm hand pressed to his head, even if the cloth it held dripped. Held? Dripped?

"I haven't seen Heaven, though I've seen a bit of Hell—that looks like blazing furnaces in the boiler room of a ship, and I should know, I've seen plenty. Why does everyone think I'm dead?" Jimmy inspected Donal's head again, apparently finding it too hard to dent. "Isn't anyone glad to see me?"

"We're glad, Jimmy, very glad." Glad was not enough of a word, if it were true; Donal felt Jimmy's fingertips on his scalp, but then, had he not wakened every night for weeks with his lover's body pressed to his and found it only a memory? "How did you survive?" Donal decided to sit up, although the answer might put him flat on the floor again. He wanted to fling himself into Jimmy's arms, damn all for propriety, but what if he went straight through?

"By lifting with me legs and not me back. One scoop for every mile the *Carmania* travelled, it's enough to kill a body." Jimmy put his hands out—his upper arms strained his sleeves, suggesting he had shoveled his way across the Atlantic twice.

"The *Carmania?*" His heart understood before his ears did—the knocking against his ribs threatened to flatten him. "What were ye doin' in a Clyde-built ship?" He let Jimmy swing him to the settee—if he was a ghost, he was a solid, strong ghost, the sort that would stay.

"Well, there was a bit of trouble." Jimmy sat next to Donal, dabbing a bit more at the tender spot. "I missed the *Titanic* in Southampton—we spent a few minutes too long at the pub, but there were all these other ships, so I thought to check out the competition. Don't think much of John Brown and Co.'s rivet spacing, I tell ye." He snapped back from inner contemplation of boiler design. "What happened?"

"Iceberg—the ship sank with more than fifteen hundred souls. Ye weren't listed as surviving or known dead. We thought you'd gone down...." Voicing his fear and seeing it unfounded, Donal watched the understanding steal the sunshine from Jimmy's brow. "None of the guarantee group has come home."

"None?" Jimmy looked to the Deegans, but there was nothing in their faces to contradict Donal's words. "Poor Alfy. He was just eighteen. There were children aboard; some little boys came down to peek at us. Fifteen hun— How many were saved?"

"Seven hundred and a few. The stories are terrifyin'." Donal had read every one, and for the last few days, the eyewitness accounts had trickled in. The Marconi operator Harold Bride's interview had brought Donal's tears again, and the passenger Dr. Washington Dodge's recounting had sent him retching out into the garden.

Jimmy drew Donal against his side and captured Mrs. Deegan with the other arm. "Ye poor things, thinking me—" Donal was glad he didn't speak the word, and would not speak or move, for that would break the magic of touching Jimmy, real, warm, and breathing. "I didn't wire—it would have taken every penny I had in me pocket, and I was back in the same time—I didn't think it would matter. She sank?"

"She sank." Donal and the Deegans repeated the impossible truth.

"How could our beautiful, unsinkable ship go down?" Jimmy fell back in the settee, crushed. "With fifteen hundred people. So many... Oh, their families..."

"But you missed the ship?" Relief made Donal retell this miracle, and he would chase Jimmy's thoughts from being a mile underwater.

"I did. So that last jar saved me life. There'll be no talk of Temperance pledges ever again, Mrs. Deegan!" Jimmy sprang to his feet, pulling Donal and the landlady with him, crushing them into a mass of arms and tears, with Mr. Deegan hopping about and thumping Jimmy's back.

Donal would forgive Mrs. Deegan's presence in the only embrace he might ever be able to give Jimmy publicly, for was not his *stór* home safe? The look they exchanged over her head made every grief fade; there would be kisses soon.

"Did I not promise I would return?"

Too softly for the Deegans to hear, Donal murmured, "Aye, *mo ghrá,* that ye did."

P.D. Singer lives in Colorado with her slightly bemused husband, two rowdy teenage boys, and thirty pounds of cats. She's a big believer in research, first-hand if possible, so the reader can be quite certain P.D. has skied down a mountain face-first, been stepped on by rodeo horses, acquired a potato burn or two, and will never, ever, write a novel that includes sky-diving.

When not writing, playing her fiddle, or skiing, she can be found with a book in hand.

Pam is always glad to hear from readers; find her at PD.Singer@live.com and follow the adventures at http://pdsinger.com.